FOREWORD

I DREW THE ROUGH DRAFT OF *MOVING DAY* IN A SKETCHBOOK DURING THE SUMMER OF 2013.
I INTENDED IT TO BE A KIND OF FRESH START FOR MY VARIOUS COMICS, BECAUSE IT'S SET
CHRONOLOGICALLY BEFORE EVERYTHING ELSE I'VE DONE. OVER THE YEARS, MANY HAVE ASKED
HOW PUZZLE AND DIAMOND GOT TOGETHER, BUT INSTEAD OF TELLING THAT STORY (I KNOW,
I'M A TEASE...), I WANTED TO SHOW THEIR RELATIONSHIP DYNAMIC AS THEY EMBARK ON ONE OF
THE BIGGEST RELATIONSHIP MILESTONES THERE IS - LIVING TOGETHER! *CUE DRAMATIC MUSIC*

I FOUND MYSELF BOGGED DOWN WITH COMMISSION WORK TO MAKE ENDS MEET, AND I HAD NO
TIME TO WORK ON COMICS. ALMOST A YEAR HAD PASSED SINCE MY PRIOR COMIC, *MISPLACED
VIRTUES*, AND I WAS LOOKING FOR A WAY TO MAKE A NEW ONE HAPPEN. I SAW THAT THIS THING
CALLED *PATREON* WAS TAKING OFF, AND I STUDIED HOW ARTISTS USED IT AND DECIDED TO GIVE
IT A GO. I NEVER WOULD HAVE IMAGINED I'D DO SO WELL WITH IT - AND I'M FLOORED BY THE
RESPONSE MY COMIC RECEIVED. WITH THE HELP OF HUNDREDS OF PLEDGERS, I WAS ABLE TO
AFFORD TO TAKE TIME AWAY FROM COMMISSION WORK TO COMPLETE THIS COMIC. I THINK IT'S
MY BEST WORK YET (THOUGH I ALWAYS SAY THAT. YOU BE THE JUDGE!).

INCLUDED IN THIS PRINT EDITION IS THE ORIGINAL 22-PAGE COMIC, PLUS PINUPS AND ALTERNATE
COVERS THAT WERE COMPLETED AT MY PATRON'S REQUESTS THROUGH VOTING POLLS AND
WORKSTREAMS. I'VE ALSO INCLUDED A FEW CONCEPT SKETCHES OF THE COVER ART THAT DIDN'T
MAKE IT TO FINAL, BUT I STILL THOUGHT WERE CUTE.

I HOPE YOU ENJOY THIS AND MY OTHER COMICS, BOTH PAST AND FUTURE. THANK YOU!

CHEERS,
KADATH

YOU GOT THAT, PUZ?
YEAH, I THINK SO...
...LET ME TRY THE HANDLE.

YOU MEAN THE KNOB?
HEE HEE, DON'T MAKE ME LAUGH, OR I'LL DROP THESE BOXES!
ALMOST...GOT IT...
THERE!

RIGHT! NOW...OH!
WOAAH, OHHH NOOOO!

CRASH

YOU ALL RIGHT, PUZ?
YEAH...
NICE VIEW.

I'M SO SORRY.
I HOPE NOTHING'S BROKEN.
IT'S OKAY LUV, ACCIDENTS HAPPEN.

OH, NO NEED TO GET ALL MISTY.
YOU'RE A KLUTZ, BUT I STILL LOVE YOU, SILLY GIRL.

BESIDES, YOU'RE NOT HURT AND THAT'S WHAT MATTERS.
I CAN REPLACE A BROKEN ITEM, BUT I COULDN'T REPLACE YOU.

HOW ABOUT SOME TEA?
MMM, YES PLEASE!

MOMENTS LATER.
STILL HAVEN'T FOUND THE TEAPOT, PUZ? AH WELL.

YOU'LL HAVE TO MAKE DO WITH NO SOY AND SUGAR.
THAT'S OKAY!

THANK YOU!

WHEN ARE WE GOING TO TACKLE THIS MESS?

UGH, IT'S OVERWHELMING. I'M TIRED JUST LOOKING AT IT!
IT DIDN'T SEEM LIKE A LOT AT MY OLD PLACE!
YOU HAVE TOO MUCH STUFF, PUZ.

SO, YOU THINK YOU'LL ENJOY LIVING HERE?

IF YOU DON'T MIND KEEPING ME AROUND!
HOPEFULLY I WON'T BREAK ANYTHING...

OF COURSE, LUV! I'M REALLY LOOKING FORWARD TO IT!
BESIDES, I LIKE HAVING SUCH FETCHING COMPANY.
OH, STOP!

4

MMMH!
ALL THIS MOVING'S WORN ME OUT. TIME FOR A SHOWER.
SOUNDS GOOD!

I WOULDN'T MIND SOME COMPANY...
OH!

THE SHOWER'S BIG ENOUGH FOR TWO.

ARE YOU SURE? I MIGHT TRIP IN THERE, TOO.

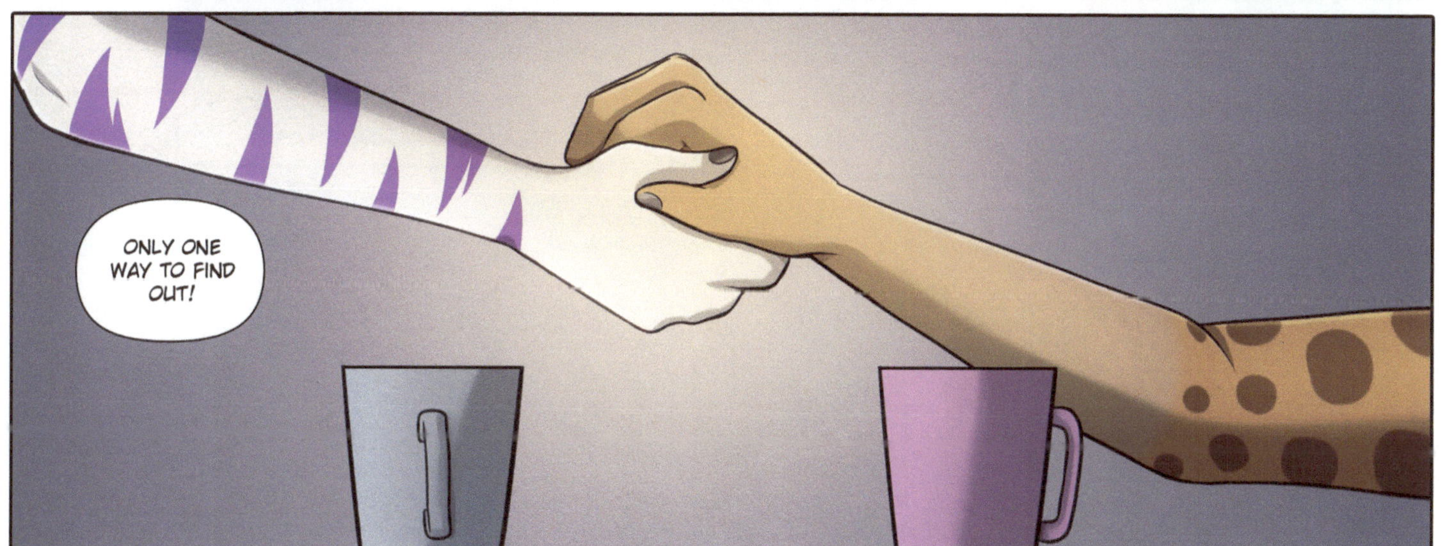

ONLY ONE WAY TO FIND OUT!

RRIIIH
OOF, CAN'T WAIT TO GET THESE DIRTY THINGS OFF!
HOLD UP, PUZ!
LET ME HELP YOU THERE.
IF YOU GET MY DRIFT...
B-BUT I'M ALL DIRTY!
SHUSH NOW, I LOVE YOU THE WAY YOU ARE.
BUT I ESPECIALLY LOVE YOU WHEN YOU'RE DIRTY.

YOU'RE SO CHEEKY, DI!
I KNOW. *MWAH!*

HMM, LET'S TAKE CARE OF THIS FIRST.
YOUR BACK MUST BE SORE.
AFTER ALL...

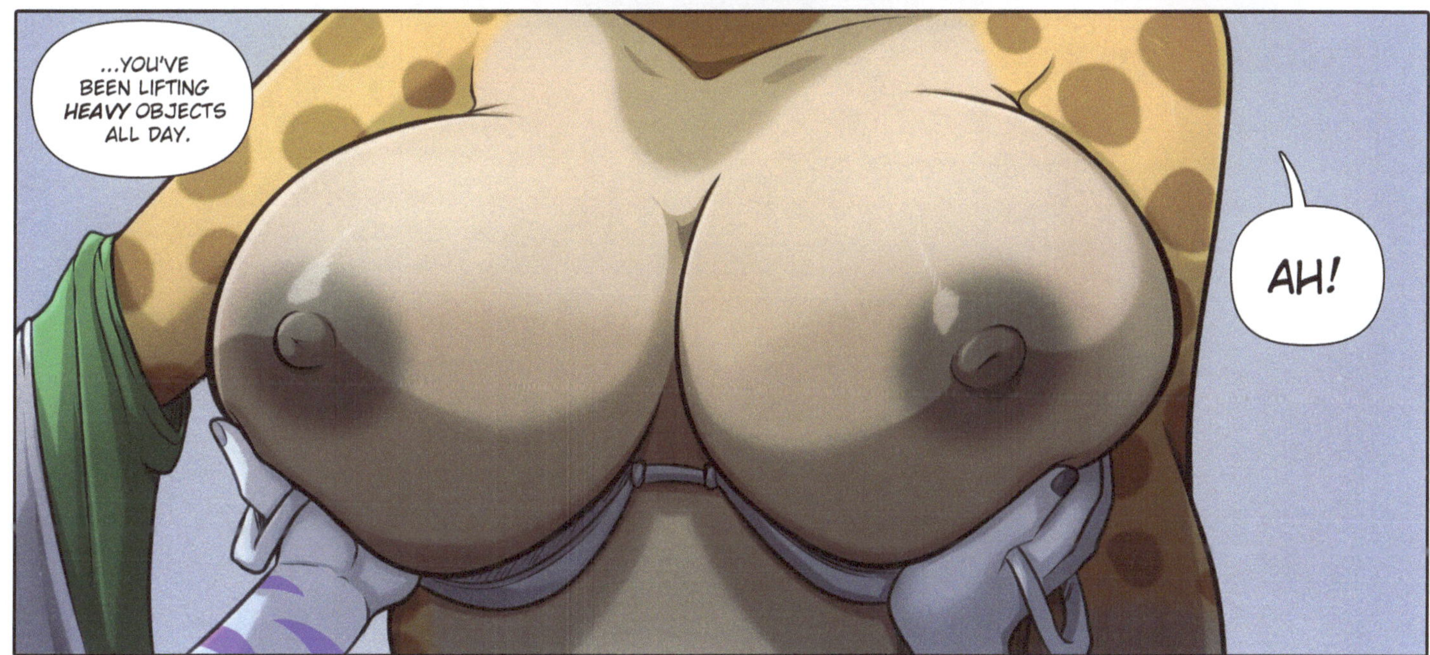

...YOU'VE BEEN LIFTING HEAVY OBJECTS ALL DAY.
AH!

REALLY PUZ, YOUR 'GIRLS' PUT MOST GIRLS' TO SHAME.

BUT THEY GIVE ME THE MOST HORRID BACK PAIN.

I'LL GIVE YOU A BACK MASSAGE LATER, BUT FIRST LET'S TREAT THESE LADIES.
THEY'VE HAD A LONG DAY.

MMM!

OOOH!

MMM.
AH!
OW!
BE GENTLE...
SORRY. *MMPH*
CAN'T HELP MYSELF.
NOW FOR THESE...
HEH, PINK LOOKS GOOD ON YOU!

CUTE KNICKERS, PUZ!
UM, DI?

THE WATER'S STILL RUNNING. IF WE WANT HOT WATER...

FINE, FINE. RUSH ME, WHY DON'T YA?
S-SORRY, I-
OH, STOP BEING DAFT AND GET IN HERE!

SORRY, I JUST DIDN'T WANT THE WATER TO GET COLD.
WELL, A COLD SHOWER DOES KILL THE MOOD.

DID YOU KNOW THAT THE AVERAGE PERSON USES *150 LITRES* OF DRINKING WATER PER DAY?
HOWEVER, AT LEAST A *THIRD* OF THAT WATER IS WASTED?

THAT'S *UTTERLY* FASCINATING.
ISN'T IT? IN FACT—
PUZ?
YES?
DO SHUT UP.

SORRY. I TEND TO RAMBLE.
I KNOW.
SNERK
WHAT NOW?

IT'S JUST...
...YOU LOOK RATHER SILLY WHEN YOUR HAIR'S WET! *SNORT* HEE HEE!

LIKE A *MOP!* HAHA!
WANT TO KNOW WHAT'S SILLIER?
W-WHAT?

YOU LEFT YOUR *KNICKERS* ON.
YEEP!

OH DEAR!
TSK TSK!

SUCH A DITZ.

I'M SO EMBARRASSED...
OH HUSH, NOW.
YOU'RE ADORABLE NO MATTER WHAT YOU DO.
NOW. C'MERE!

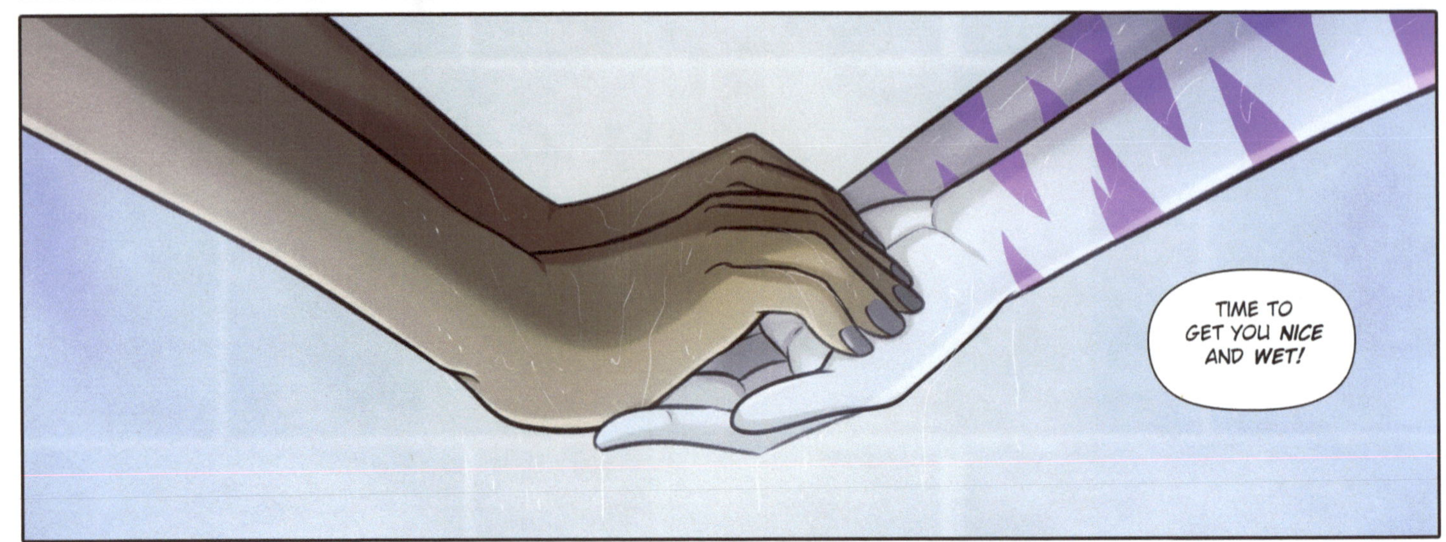

TIME TO GET YOU NICE AND WET!

AH!
AH!
AH!!
MY MY.
LOOK AT
YOU.
PRACTICALLY
TAKING MY WHOLE
HAND!
SHLP
SHLP
SHLP
SO
NICE AND
WET...
OH GOD!

PSHHHH
AAAH~ OOH, GOD!
OH DI, I'M...

I'M... I'M GOING TO CUM!
MMM - YES! I'M...NNNH!
MMMNH!
MMM, THAT'S MY GIRL!
SHLP SHLP SHLP SHLP

AHNN~ HHH!

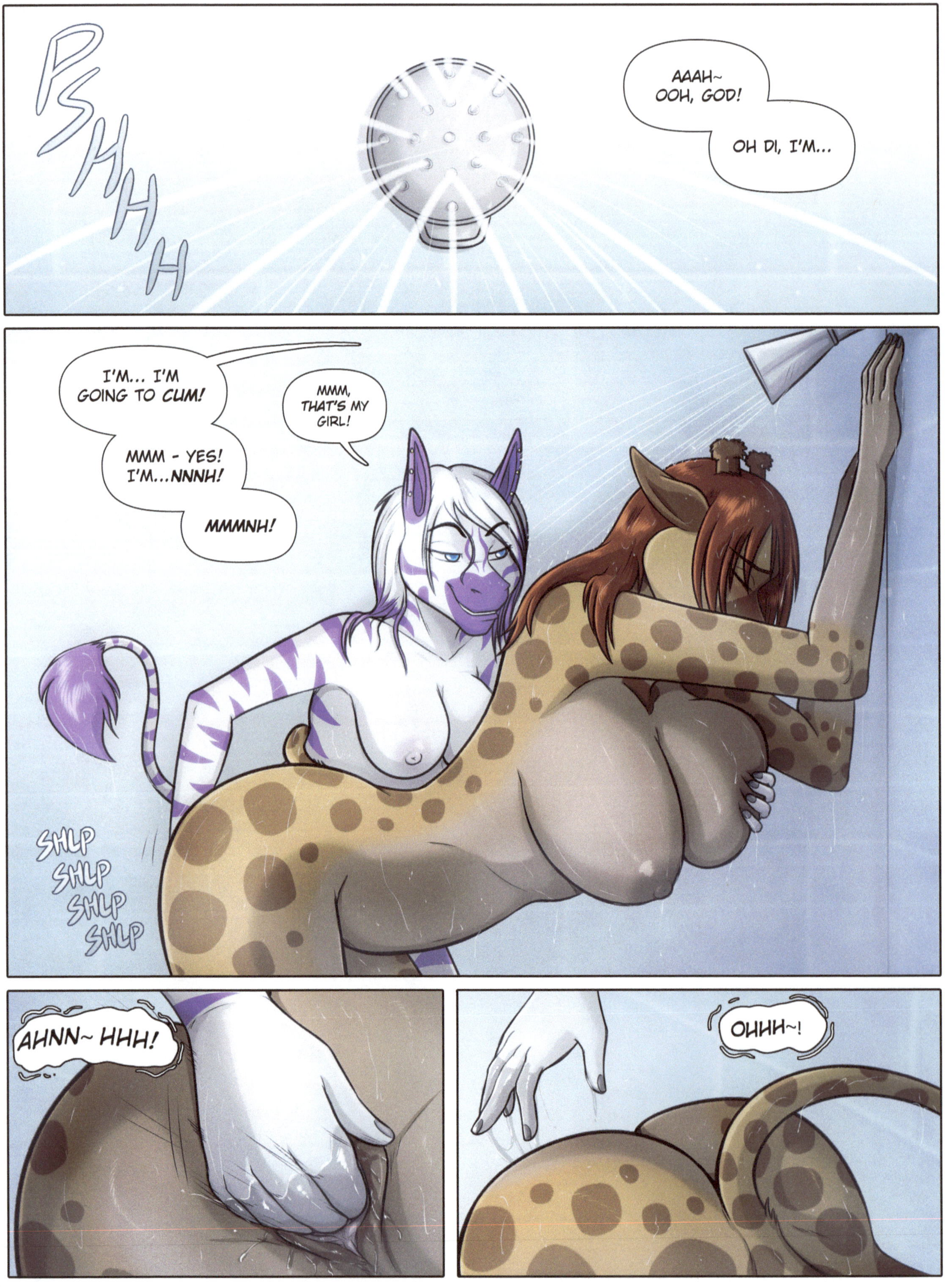

OHHH~!

14

WELL, THEN!
NOW THAT WE'RE ALL CLEANED UP...
~NIP

LET'S DRY OFF AND HEAD TO THE BEDROOM.
G-GIVE ME A MOMENT...
...M-MY LEGS ARE STILL SHAKING...

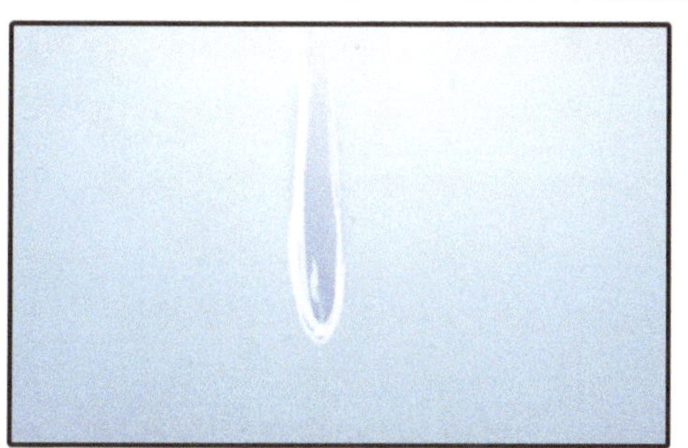

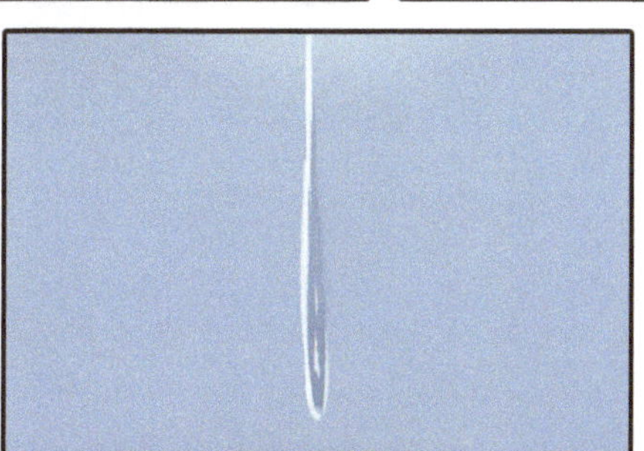

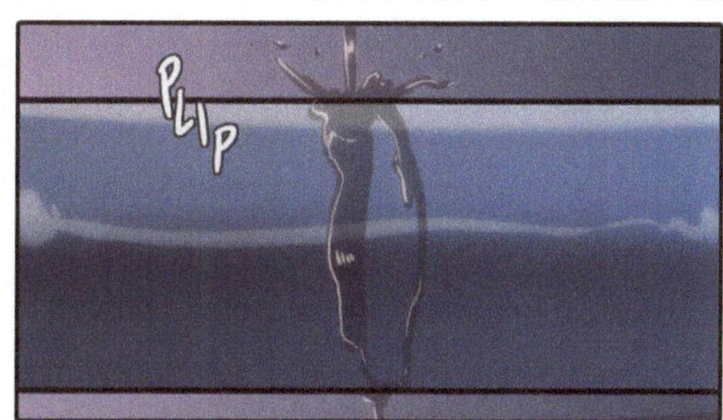

PLIP

OH MY, DI.
THAT'S AWFULLY BIG!
DON'T WORRY, THAT'S WHY I UNPACKED THE LUBE.

JUST BE GENTLE.
I'M SORE FROM MOVING ALL THOSE BOXES.
WELL THIS WAS YOUR IDEA.
I'LL GO NIIICE...
...AND EASY.
BUT DON'T WORRY.
SMLP

MMH! W-WAIT!
AREN'T YOU FORGETTING SOMETHING?

OH, RIGHT!
SORRY LUV, I WAS GETTING AHEAD OF MYSELF.

NOW, MOVE YOUR CUTE ARSE.
NO, LIFT UP.
THERE YOU GO!

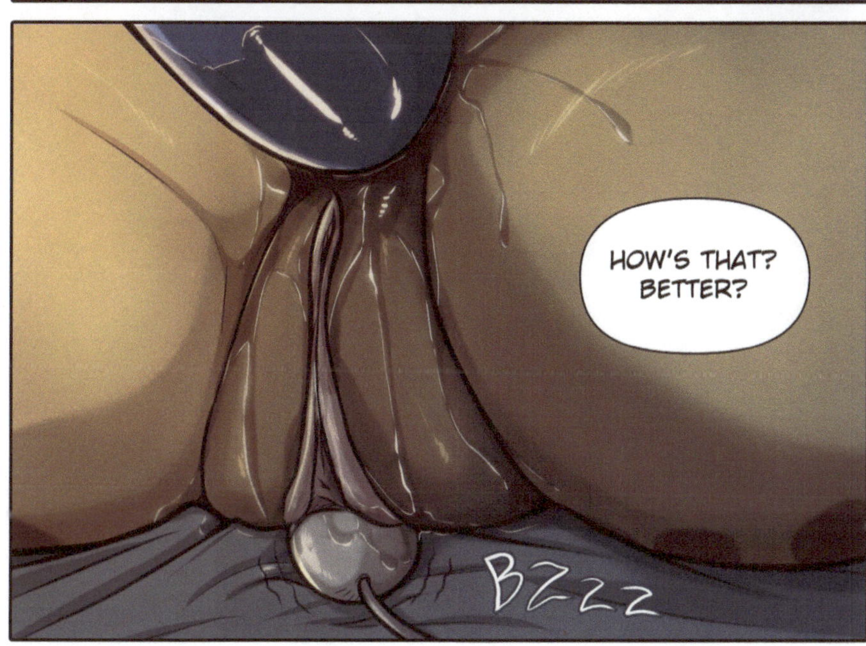

HOW'S THAT? BETTER?
BZZZ

OOH, MUCH BETTER!

SHALL WE CONTINUE?

MMHM!

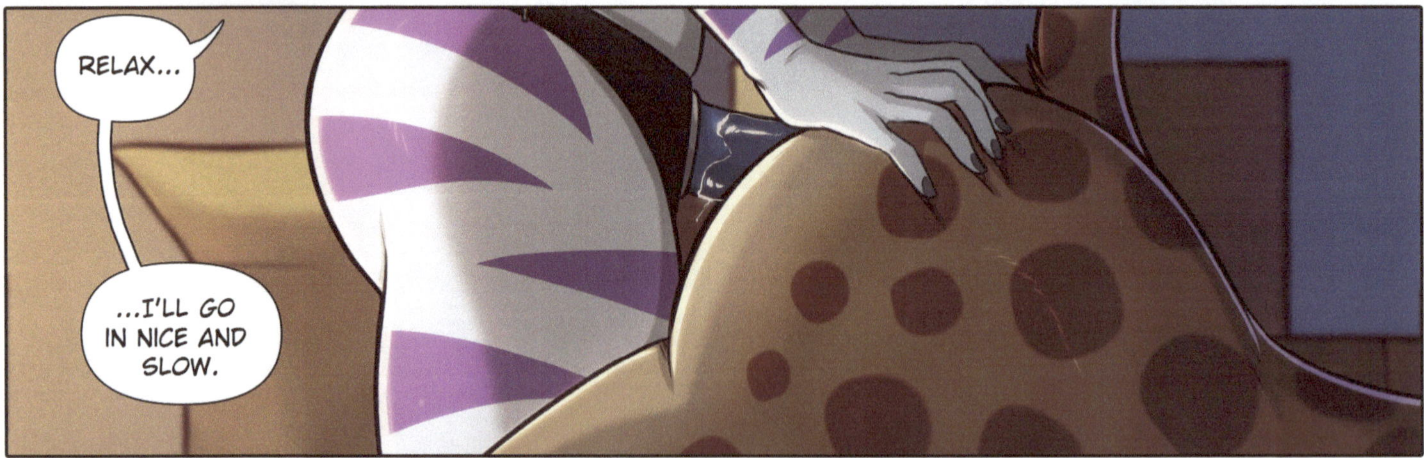

RELAX...
...I'LL GO IN NICE AND SLOW.

MMM, THAT'S MY GIRL!
GOODNESS, ALL THE WAY TO THE HILT!

HOW'S THAT FEEL?
WANT ME TO GO FASTER?
RIGHT. BRACE YOURSELF, BEAUTIFUL!
AH! REALLY GOOD!
MMHM!
AH!!

SHLL~

~PLAP!

AH! OH GOD, DI!
YES! HARDER!
PLAP
PLAP
PLAP
PLAP

PLAP
PLAP
PLAP
BZZZ
DI! DI, I'M GOING TO CUM!

AHHHNN~!!

MMM, I KNEW FROM THE MOMENT I MET YOU...

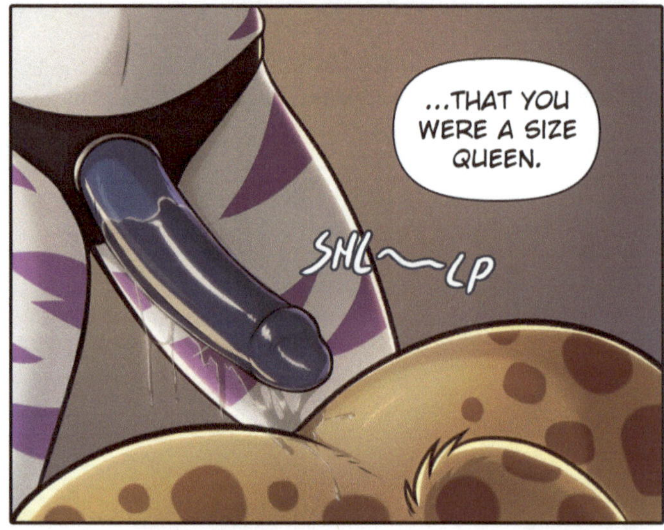

...THAT YOU WERE A SIZE QUEEN.
SHL~LP

W-WELL, I AM BIGGER THAN MOST GIRLS.

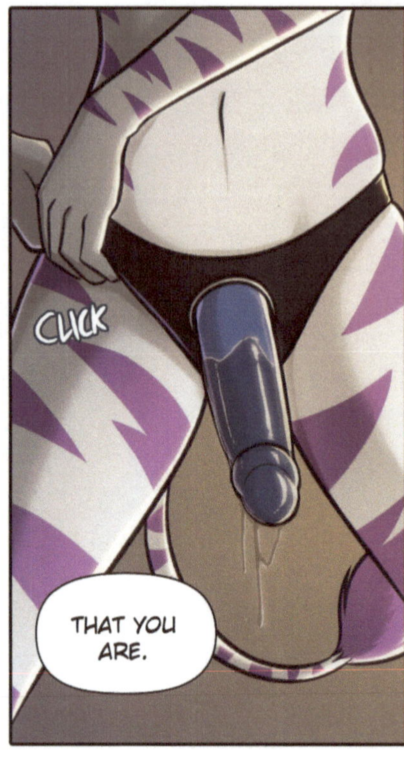

CLICK
THAT YOU ARE.

YOU KNOW WHAT ELSE ABOUT YOU IS BIG?

MY B-
YOUR BIG, BEAUTIFUL TONGUE.
MMM!
NOW PUT IT TO GOOD USE!

LET'S SWITCH PLACES.

OOOH!
AHHH!

AHH!
YES!
SHLP SHLP

GOD, PUZ!
YOUR TONGUE IS INCREDIBLE!

MMM~!

SLCH
SLCH
OH GOD!

R-RIGHT THERE...!
YES! YES!!

I'M GONNA~!

AHHH!
NNN~ AHHHNN!!

GOD, PUZ.
YOU MAKE ME CUM LIKE I NEVER HAVE BEFORE.

I'M HAPPY YOU THINK SO.
THINK? IT'S AN UNDISPUTED FACT. YOU SHOULD PATENT THAT TONGUE!

SO... READY TO FINISH UNPACKING?
HOW ABOUT FIRST THING TOMORROW MORNING?
YOU WORE ME OUT.

HEY DI?
THINK I'LL BE A GOOD FLATMATE?
OF COURSE LUV! I'M GOING TO ENJOY YOUR COMPANY.
THE END

BRRR!

DI, YOU SAID THIS WAS THE LATEST FASHION TREND, BUT IT SEEMS REALLY IMPRACTICAL!

SNICKER

FASHION'S NOT ABOUT COMFORT, LUV!

Happy Holidays

COVER SKETCH CONCEPT 1

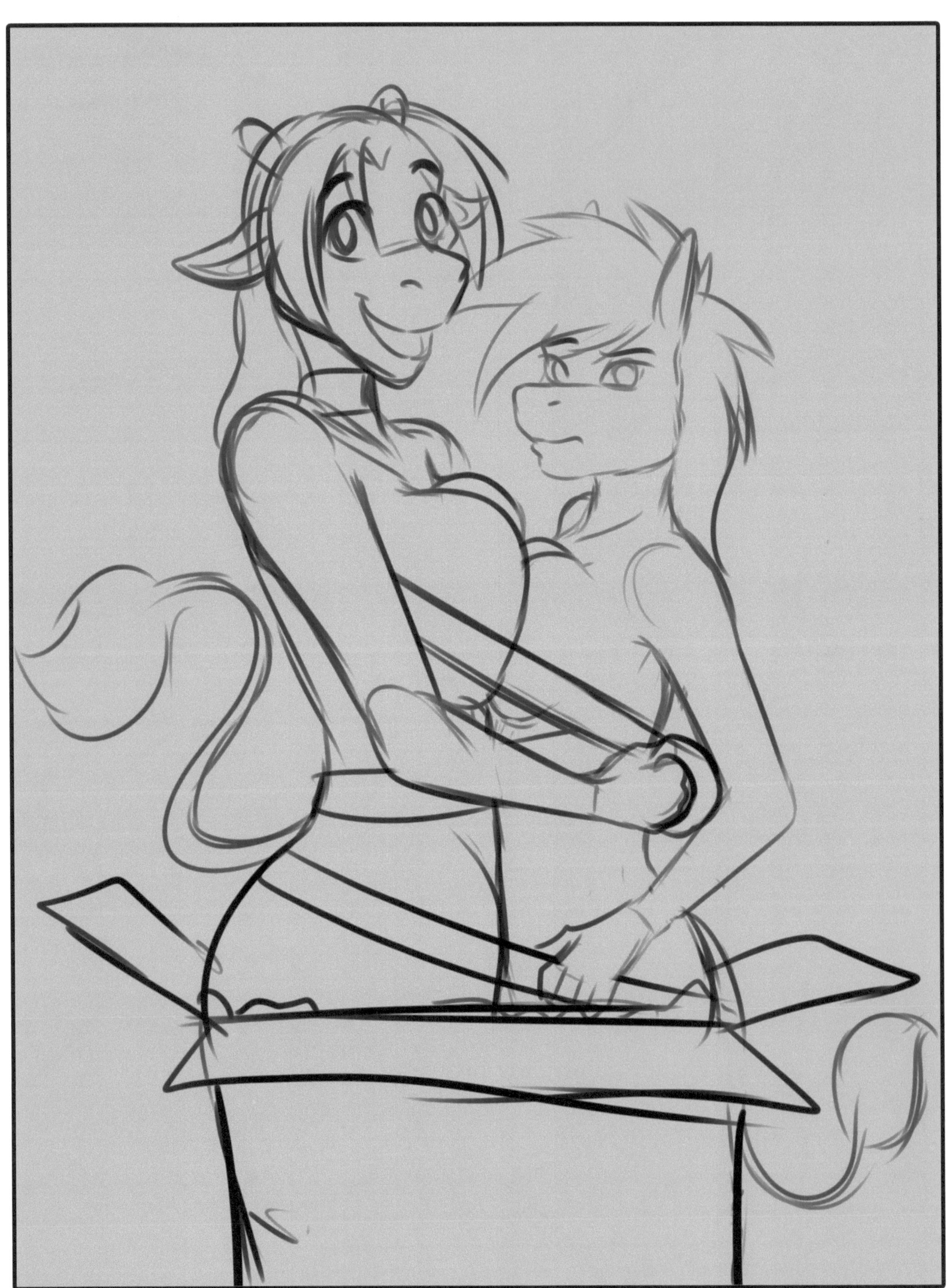
COVER SKETCH CONCEPT 2

SPECIAL THANKS

THIS COMIC WAS MADE POSSIBLE BY THE GENEROUS SUPPORT FROM PLEDGERS ON PATREON.
WHILE ALL OF THEM HAVE MY HEARTFELT THANKS, THE FOLLOWING PATRONS DESERVE
SPECIAL RECOGNITION:

ANEURIN RICHARDS
ARCENAUX
ASHDUDE
BRANDON MCBRIDE
CYNFALL
DAVID JONES
ERIN BARNES
FIRESTORM3
GRRXMASTER
HAMMERUK9
ILANTERN
ISIAH JACOBS
JASON ROSS
JONATHAN SMOOT
JWT
KAUL AGAROUS
MAJINKOBA
LEGION
PSYDRAGGY
ROBERT GRIFFIN
SQUIDLORDOFSQUIDS
WILLIAM BURLIN
WILLIAM HOLIFIELD
ZEROSM

I'D ALSO LIKE TO SPECIFICALLY THANK THE FOLLOWING:

KAYLII – FOR YOUR UNWAVERING LOVE AND SUPPORT (AND REDLINES!)

FURPLANET – FOR THE LOVELY PRINT EDITION OF THIS COMIC

BRENT – FOR BUSINESS ADVICE AND LATENIGHTGRIND HELP

PATREON – FOR ALLOWING ME THE OPPORTUNITY TO MAKE THIS HAPPEN

THANK YOU ALL SO MUCH!

Late Night
GRIND.com
Adult Anthropomorphic
Art & Comics
Check out more at:
www.LateNightGrind.com

BadDogBooks.com
FUR-EBOOKS AND COMICS
FEATURING BRAFORD, CYANNI, FURIOUS, KEVIN FRANE,
KYELL GOLD, RECHAN, RUKIS ...AND MANY MORE!